Big City Magic

Uncover the Secret of the Big Apple

by Jeanne Bender
illustrated by Kate Willows

PINA PUBLISHING SEATTLE

PINA PUBLISHING SEATTLE

 First edition, 2019

For information about special discounts for bulk purchases contact: lindielou.com/contact-us.html

Manufactured in the United States of America
Library of Congress Cataloging-in-Publication Data Bender, Jeanne

Summary:

Lindie Lou can hardly wait to see what adventures New York City has to offer. She hears a legend about a Big Apple Tree located somewhere on Manhattan Island. The legend says that if you find the tree, you'll discover the biggest, sweetest, juiciest apples on earth.

A rescue puppy named Bella, agrees to help Lindie Lou search for the Big Apple Tree. During their quest, they encounter some unusual characters including a mysterious wise woman, a curious pack of dogs, an energetic restaurant owner, and a jolly mentor.

Follow Lindie Lou on an incredible journey to find the Big Apple Tree because there's more to the story. The legend also says… "This tree holds a secret so amazing, so incredible, and so important, it can change your life!"

ISBN: 978-1-943493-27-2 (hardcover)
ISBN: 978-1-943493-26-5 (softcover)
ISBN: 978-1-943493-28-9 (e-book)

[1. Adventure Stories. 2. Pets–Fiction. 3. Dogs–Fiction. 4. Fall-Fiction. 5. Travel-Fiction. 6. Juvenile-Fiction. 7. Thanksgiving-Fiction. 8. Legends-Fiction. 9. Friendship-Fiction. 10. Travel-Fiction. 11. New York City-Fiction.]

Dedicated to New York City.
A one-of-a-kind metropolis
worth discovering and uncovering.
A city whose ecological footprint
is admirable, where diversity thrives and
neighborhoods take on their own unique identity.
What's not to love?

A special mention of my dear friend
Maria Ferrer, who lived in New York City as a child
and shared her favorite memories with me.

A special thanks to the
Central Park Conservancy for their
tireless efforts to keep Central Park
clean, safe, and beautiful.

Lindie Lou®

Uncovering a secret is hard to do,
a difficult task for Lindie Lou.
While following clues around New York City,
she doesn't give up or ask for pity.
The secret is not what she thought it would be,
But. . . it changes her life, as you will see.

–Jeanne Bender

Here's what kids told Jeanne Bender about Lindie Lou:

I like when Lindie Lou flies in the airplanes. It makes me want to fly too. I really like to explore new places. I'd like to go to Central Park just like Lindie Lou does in Big City Magic.

—Sophia, age 5

We like Lindie Lou. She is a funny dog. We are really anxious for book 4 and can't wait to hear more about Max and Lindie Lou's siblings. We love your books!

—Mrs. Lambert's 2nd grade class

I think the Lindie Lou books are really cool because Lindie Lou and her family go on real adventures to real places that we can go to with our family. I also really like that we get to know how Lindie Lou's brother and sister puppies are doing.

—Ellington, age 7

My daughter Hayden loves the Lindie Lou books. Even though she is only 3½ she is hooked! We have the poster hanging next to her bed. She asks me to tell her the names of all the puppies. This morning when she woke up she said, "Mommy, I dreamt about Lindie Lou and the puppies!"

—Kayla (mom) and Hayden, age 3½

DIAMOND
JASPER
RUBY
TOPAZ
LL
LindieLou.com

Kate

Bryan

Gundula

Leeza

Tomas

Bella

Brody Saul Moe Mika

Petra

Tony

Maria

Kris

Contents

Chapter 1

WE'RE ALMOST THERE

Lindie Lou looked out of the window. She was on an airplane. This time she was allowed to sit on Kate's lap. Kate was her owner and made her feel safe.

Lindie Lou liked to ride on airplanes. It was fun to *fly* across the sky. She also liked being near the clouds. But most of all, Lindie Lou liked airplanes because they are fast.

We're on our next adventure, thought Lindie Lou. She LOVED adventures. She also loved to travel. When she was out in the world, she met many new people and learned a lot of new things.

The airplane was flying above the clouds. Up here, the sky was blue and the sun was shining. Lindie

Lou liked to look for shapes in the clouds. Today the clouds looked like a

blanket.

Lindie Lou closed her eyes. She thought about what it would be like if she had wings and could fly.

I wonder how fast we're going, thought Lindie Lou. She could hear the airplane's engines humming. Lindie Lou opened her eyes and looked around. *I wonder where the engines are.*

Kate stretched out her arms and gave Lindie Lou a **big squeeze.** She was happy they were traveling together.

Lindie Lou is fun to travel with, thought Kate. *She's calm, quiet, and cuddly.* Kate hugged Lindie Lou again.

"We're almost there," said Bryan. He was Kate's husband. Bryan reached over and tickled Lindie Lou on the top of her head.

The airplane tipped down and flew under the clouds.

"Look," said Kate. "There's the New York City skyline."

Bryan leaned over and looked out of the window.

"The buildings are even taller than the ones in Seattle where we live," said Bryan.

"Agreed," said Kate. "Can you see the two rivers on either side of Manhattan Island?"

"I sure can," said Bryan. "The Hudson is on the left and the East River is on the right."

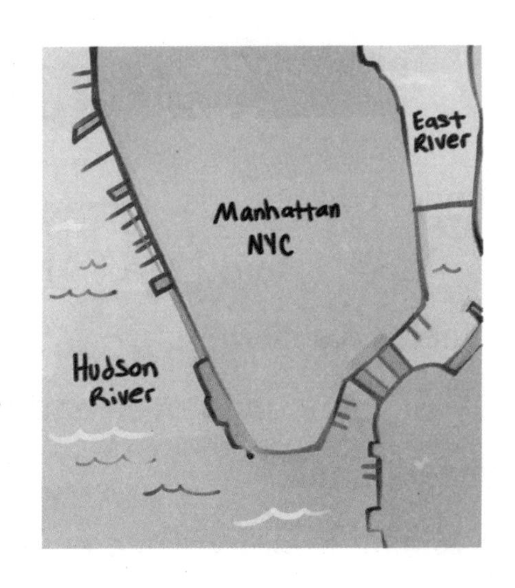

"Exactly," said Kate.

The airplane made a **wide** turn.

"Look," said Kate. "I can see the Statue of Liberty."

"I see it too," said Bryan. "She is beautiful."

"She reminds me of our freedom," said Kate.

"She sure does," replied Bryan.

What is freedom? thought Lindie Lou. *I think freedom means. . . I can go anywhere I want without being on a leash. But then I have to be very careful not to get into any trouble.*

Lindie Lou looked at the Statue of Liberty.

Freedom must be very important, if someone made a statue to remind us of it, thought Lindie Lou.

The airplane flew closer to the ground.

"Good afternoon," said a man with a **loud** voice. The sound was coming from a speaker. "Please prepare for landing. Make sure your seat belts are on and everything is stowed away."

"Time for you to go into your travel cart," said Kate. She lifted Lindie Lou off her lap and set her on the floor. Lindie Lou crawled inside her travel cart, turned around, and lay down. She knew she would be safer there during landing.

Kate reached over and held Bryan's hand.

"I'm looking forward to showing Leeza the drawings I made for her new book."

"I think they're great," said Bryan. He smiled at Kate.

A few minutes later, Lindie Lou heard a loud **THUD** when the plane landed.

I can't wait to see where we are, thought Lindie Lou. *I heard Kate call this place New York City.*

Lindie Lou jumped up on Kate's lap. She looked out of the window. The airplane was moving very slowly now and the airport building was far away.

Lindie Lou closed her eyes, rested her head on her huge front paws, and smiled.

Chapter 2

THE BIG APPLE

When the airplane stopped and the door opened, Kate and Bryan followed the other passengers off the airplane. Lindie Lou was back in her travel cart on wheels. They stepped onto a moving walkway that took them through the airport. It ended at the baggage claim area.

This part of the airport reminds me of my friend Max, thought Lindie Lou. She missed her wise friend but knew she would see him when she returned to Seattle.

Bryan and Kate picked up their luggage and stepped onto another

moving

walkway. This one took them outside of the building.

A cool November **breeze** blew against their faces. Kate buttoned up her coat. They walked toward a row of colorful car pods.

The trees around the airport were covered in red, yellow, and orange leaves. Lindie Lou closed her eyes and sniffed the air.

Hmm, thought Lindie Lou, *these trees look and smell just like the ones in Saint Louis, where I was born.*

"There's our name," said Bryan.

The word KELLY blinked in the window of a white-and-purple car pod.

Bryan put their suitcases in the back and closed the hatch. Kate jumped into one of the seats. Lindie Lou was still in her travel cart. Kate lifted the cart up and set it by her feet.

Bryan sat next to Kate. He pushed a button, and the doors closed. Two safety belts reached around their laps and clicked into place. Kate touched the screen in front of her.

"Hello," said a friendly voice.

"Could you please take us to. . . One West 72nd Street?" asked Kate.

"Sure," replied the voice. "The ride will take fifty-five minutes. We'll travel north through Queens, past East Harlem, and end up on the west side of Manhattan."

"Okay," said Kate.

"Please call me Blue," said the voice. "I was named after the color of New York's state bird."

"It's nice to meet you, Blue," said Bryan.

The car pod drove away from the airport and onto a freeway. Kate and Bryan looked up at the tall buildings.

"I heard the nickname for New York City is the Big Apple," said Bryan.

"The Big Apple?" asked Kate. "What a strange name." She looked at the screen. "Blue, where does the name the *Big Apple* come from?"

A picture of an apple tree appeared on the screen.

"The Big Apple is New York's state fruit. It grows on apple trees. Apples come in many different colors. The most common are red, green, and yellow. Apples are crisp and taste sweet, but they are sometimes sour."

Kate and Bryan laughed.

"I'm sure Tomas and Leeza know why New York City is called the Big Apple," said Kate.

"Are they waiting for us at their apartment?" asked Bryan.

"Yes," replied Kate. "Leeza said their home is across the street from Central Park."

"Nice," answered Bryan.

A park? thought Lindie Lou. *I love parks!* She remembered playing

the Chase Game

in the park at the bottom of the Space Needle in Seattle.

"Did you say Tomas and Leeza have a dog?" asked Bryan.

"Yes," replied Kate. "Her name is Bella. She's a six-month-old rescue puppy."

A puppy? thought Lindie Lou. *Awesome! I can't wait to meet her.* She **wiggled** her tail.

The car pod drove for many miles. After several turns, it pulled off the road and entered a driveway.

A man in a gray uniform was waiting for them. Bryan pushed a button, and the car pod's doors opened.

"Welcome to the

Gray
Stone
Manor,"

said the man.

Kate reached down and lifted Lindie Lou out of her travel cart. Lindie Lou looked up at the building in front of them. Something made her. . .

growl.

Chapter 3

DO YOU SEE WHAT I SEE?

Kate, Bryan, and Lindie Lou stepped out of the car pod. They looked up at the building in front of them. It was trimmed in gray stones just like the driveway. Steep stone steps led up to a pair of dark-brown doors. In the middle of the doors were two shiny brass lion heads. The lions had round brass door knockers in their mouths.

"Do you see what I see?" asked Bryan. "Look at the sides of the doors."

Two green marble pillars stood on either side of the doors. On top of the pillars were giant gray stone dragons. The dragons were looking down at them.

Kate gasped, and then she looked at Lindie Lou.

"Were you growling at those dragons?" asked Kate.

"Maybe she was growling at what's above them," said Bryan.

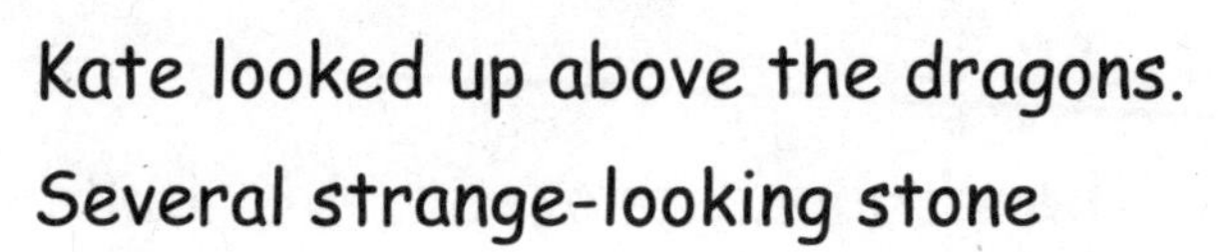

Kate looked up above the dragons. Several strange-looking stone

creatures looked down at them. They had their mouths open, and their tongues were sticking out.

"What are those things?" asked Kate.

"Gargoyles," said the man in the gray uniform. "They actually serve a purpose. They're attached to the ends of the rain gutters and direct water away from the building."

"Then what are the dragons for?" asked Kate.

"The dragons protect this building and the people who live inside."

"Well, they made our puppy dog growl," said Kate. She reached down and picked up Lindie Lou.

"Don't worry," said the man. "Those stone dragons won't harm you or your puppy. I've worked here for over twenty years, and I haven't seen them hurt anyone."

"Good to know," said Kate. She held Lindie Lou tight and followed Bryan up the steep gray stone steps.

The doors automatically slid open. Bryan was the first to walk inside. Kate and Lindie Lou followed him into the Gray Stone Manor.

Chapter 4

MAY I HELP YOU?

Bryan, Kate, and Lindie Lou walked down a long dim hallway. They could see a green light at the other end. Their footsteps echoed on the gray stone floor. When they reached the other end of the hall, they peeked around the corner.

Giant green apple trees were painted on the walls. Their branches reached up toward the ceiling. The ceiling had a glass dome in the center. Images of branches, leaves, and apples were painted on the dome. The light from the dome gave the room a soft green glow.

"This room is *beautiful*," said Kate. She entered the room then turned in a circle so she could see everything.

"Someone sure likes apple trees," said Bryan.

There was a large desk across the room. A woman was sitting quietly behind the desk.

"How may I help you?" asked the woman. She spoke in a very deep voice. The light from the glass dome ceiling made her face look green.

Bryan walked over and read the nameplate on her desk.

"Gun-du-la?" asked Bryan.

She crossed her hands and shook her head.

"It's Goon-du-la."

"It is nice to meet you, Goon-du-la," said Bryan.

Kate approached the desk. "Hello," said Kate. "We are guests of Tomas and Leeza Rand. Our names are Kate and Bryan Kelly."

"Please sit down," said Gundula.

Bryan and Kate sat down on red leather armchairs in front of Gundula's desk. Kate held Lindie Lou on her lap.

Gundula never took her **eyes** off Kate, Bryan, or Lindie Lou. She

s l o w l y raised

her hand. Then she reached over and pushed a button on a device attached to her wrist.

"This is Leeza," came a cheerful voice from Gundula's wristband.

"Are you expecting guests?" asked Gundula.

"Yes," replied Leeza. "Their names are Kate and Bryan Kelly."

"Very well," said Gundula. "I'll send them up."

Gundula reached over and picked up a strange-looking pen. It had a

attached to the end. She handed the

pen to Bryan. Then she opened a blue leather-bound book, and slid it toward Bryan.

"Write your names in here," said Gundula. She looked at Lindie Lou. "Write your puppy dog's name in here, too."

"My pleasure," replied Bryan.

Lindie Lou looked into Gundula's eyes. They were a

bright green

color, just like hers. Gundula looked back at Lindie Lou and nodded.

"**L-I-N-D-I-E L-O-U** spells Lindie Lou," said Bryan.

Gundula reached over, picked up the book, and looked at the names. Then she raised her arm and pointed to an archway behind her.

"Walk through that archway and

follow the hallway until you reach an elevator," said Gundula. "It will take you up to the eighth floor. Don't worry about your luggage. I'll have it delivered shortly."

"Thank you," said Bryan.

Kate and Bryan stood up. Lindie Lou jumped down onto the floor. They thanked Gundula and walked toward the archway.

Lindie Lou turned and looked at Gundula.

Gundula smiled at Lindie Lou and winked.

Does she know what I'm thinking? wondered Lindie Lou.

Chapter 5

LEEZA & BELLA

Bryan, Kate, and Lindie Lou walked through the archway. Dim candlelights led them down a dark hallway. They could see a shiny brass elevator. When they reached the end of the hall, the doors slid open.

Bryan walked into the elevator. Kate and Lindie Lou followed. The doors closed very slowly. They watched the number eight light up on the wall of the elevator. When the elevator reached the eighth floor, the doors opened.

Bryan, Kate, and Lindie Lou stepped onto a soft carpet. They looked around the upstairs hallway. Many large paintings hung on the walls. All of them were framed in gold and lit with spotlights.

"These paintings look very old," said Kate. "I bet they've been here for a long time."

"Look at this one," said Bryan.

Kate walked over to Bryan.

"It looks like Gundula," said Kate.

Gundula looked much younger in the painting. She was sitting on a wooden bench next to an apple tree.

Kate gasped. "Look at the puppy sitting on Gundula's lap."

"It looks like Lindie Lou," said Bryan.

That's strange, thought Lindie Lou. *I wonder who the puppy is.*

The door at the end of the hall swung open. A woman rushed out.

She was wearing a brightly colored dress.

"It's Leeza," said Kate. She hurried down the hall. Lindie Lou and Bryan followed.

Leeza grabbed Kate and gave her a big hug. Then she looked at Bryan.

"You must be Bryan," said Leeza.

Bryan smiled and reached out his hand.

"May I have a hug?" asked Leeza.

"Of course," said Bryan

She grabbed Bryan and gave him a

"Is this little Lindie Lou?" asked Leeza. She bent down and tickled Lindie Lou under her chin. Lindie Lou closed her eyes and smiled.

"Yes," replied Kate.

"Well, you sure are a **sweetie**," said Leeza. "Would you like to meet Bella?"

Lindie Lou opened her eyes and looked through the open door.

"Follow me," said Leeza.

Leeza showed Kate and Bryan into the apartment. They took their coats off. Leeza hung them in the closet. Lindie Lou walked into the apartment.

Leeza opened a door and Bella ran out. She went over to Lindie Lou and sniffed her. Then she jumped on her. The two puppies rolled around on the floor like a couple of kids.

"Look, they're friends already," said Leeza.

"Sure looks like it," said Bryan.

"Your apartment is amazing," said Kate.

Brightly colored, modern pictures hung on the walls. A yellow, aqua, and lime-green rug lit up the living room floor. A blue-and-purple sofa and matching chairs sat in a

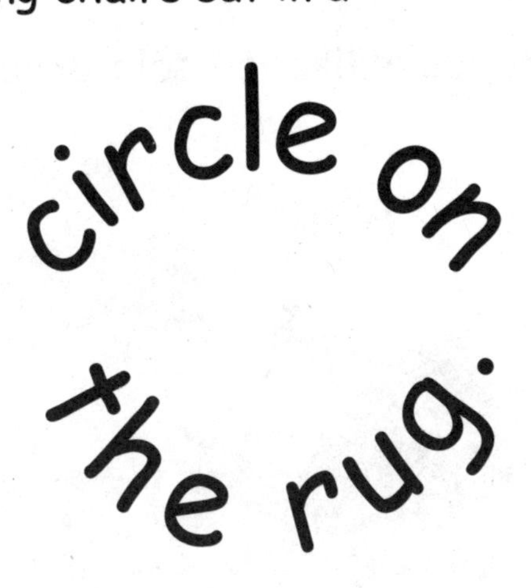

The living room and dining room were on the left, and the kitchen was on the right. In the middle of the room was a wide hallway that led to the bedrooms. But the coolest sight of all was a long white Plexiglas bench sitting in front of three giant bay windows.

"What a place," said Bryan. He walked over to the windows and looked at the view. "Central Park is even

larger

and more

beautiful

than I imagined."

Leeza and Kate walked over and sat down on the bench by the window. Bella and Lindie Lou jumped up between them.

They enjoyed the view for a while. Then Leeza turned to Bryan.

"Would you like to take an early morning jog around the park tomorrow?" asked Leeza.

"Oh boy, yes," replied Bryan.

"Okay," said Leeza. "Then you'll need a good night's sleep. Let me show you to your bedroom."

Chapter 6

NEW FRIENDS

Leeza and Bella led Kate, Bryan, and Lindie Lou down the hallway. Bella stopped at one of the bedroom doors. She was trained not to go inside unless she was told it was okay.

"You may enter," said Leeza. Bella ran into the room and sat down on the floor near the bed. Lindie Lou did the same.

"Look how well they're getting along," said Kate.

Bryan nodded.

"I LOVE the bright colors in this room," said Bryan.

"I'm glad you like it," said Leeza. She pulled open a pair of orange, yellow, and blue-striped drapes. "Take a look at the view."

"Wow," said Kate. "The trees are so colorful."

"This is the time of the year when we like to walk in the park and collect leaves. They look great on top of our holiday gifts." She turned to Bryan.

"Does Lindie Lou have an urban off-leash permit? If so, she can go anywhere in the city.

"Yes," replied Bryan.

"Does she wear a tracking device so we can locate her when she's not with us?"

"She sure does," said Bryan.

"Good, then Bella and Lindie Lou can go out on their own tomorrow."

Leeza turned to Kate.

"I'm looking forward to working with you on my new book. I can't wait to see the drawings you've created."

"I already have many to show you," said Kate.

"Wonderful," said Leeza. She walked over to Bryan. "Tomas would like to invite you to go to work with him tomorrow. He works on Wall Street. Would you like to go?"

"Yes, I would," replied Bryan.

"Okay," said Leeza. "Well, I better leave so you can unpack. Tomas will be home soon. When he arrives, we'll all have dinner."

During dinner, Kate, Bryan, Leeza, and Tomas talked about what it was like living in New York City. Tomas and Leeza told them about their favorite places to visit. Lindie Lou and Bella were

z z Z *sound asleep* z z Z

underneath the table.

After dinner, the couples sat in the living room. They made plans for the next few days. Then everyone went to their bedrooms.

Leeza brought Lindie Lou a doggie bed. She placed it in the corner near the window. Lindie Lou climbed inside and lay down. She rested her head on a soft, FUZZY PILLOW. Soon she was sound asleep, dreaming about her favorite food. . .

POPCORN!

Chapter 7

A STRANGE NOISE

Early the next morning, Lindie Lou heard a strange noise coming from a gap underneath the bedroom door.

Sniff, sniff, sniff.

Lindie Lou looked over and saw a nose poking up from under the door. She jumped up and ran to the door. The nose

disappeared. Lindie Lou whimpered. She heard another whimper on the other side of the door. Then Bella's nose appeared again.

Sniff, sniff, sniff.

"I think Bella wants to play," said Bryan. "Would you like to go out?"

Lindie Lou ran around in a circle, looked down at the gap under the door, and **barked.** Bryan sat up, stretched out his arms, and **wiggled** his fingers.

"Okay, girl. I'm coming," said Bryan.

He rolled off the bed, put on a robe, and opened the door.

Bella jumped up and ran down the hall. Lindie Lou ran after her.

Bella was a clumsy puppy with short tan fur and a big head. She had small floppy ears and a friendly face. Her legs were too long for her body. When she ran, her paws flopped around like they were loose. Lindie Lou liked her playful new friend.

Bryan followed the puppies into the kitchen. Bella and Lindie Lou ran past Leeza and out through a doggie door in the wall.

"Good morning, Leeza," said Bryan.

"Good morning," replied Leeza. "Breakfast will be ready in an hour." She was cutting up an apple.

"I can't wait to get another look at Central Park," said Bryan. He walked over to the window.

Tomas came into the kitchen and gave Leeza a morning hug. He picked up two apples and walked over to Bryan.

"Forty million people visit Central Park every year," said Tomas. He tossed Bryan an

apple. "The park is a runner's dream."
Tomas took a bite of his apple, turned, and looked out the window. "There are several jogging trails in the park. If you'd like, I'll show you some."

"That would be great," said Bryan. "I brought running clothes."

"Okay, let's get into the proper gear and meet back here in ten minutes," said Tomas. "After our jog, we'll have some breakfast, and then we can hit the Street."

"He means Wall Street," said Leeza. She smiled.

"Cool," replied Bryan. "I can't wait to see you in action."

Tomas gave Bryan a thumbs-up. Then they both left the room.

Bella and Lindie Lou ran into the kitchen and sat down at Leeza's feet.

"Good morning," said Kate. She walked in and sat down at the kitchen table.

"Good morning. Did you sleep well?" asked Leeza.

"Yes, I did," said Kate.

"Great," replied Leeza. "Take a look at this." She held up a piece of apple.

"You're just in time for our daily show."

Chapter 8

THE LEGEND OF THE BIG APPLE

"Bella, sit," said Leeza.

Bella sat down on the kitchen floor. Leeza placed a small piece of apple on top of Bella's head.

"Careful," said Leeza. "W a i t ."

Bella didn't move.

"Okay, roll over."

Bella rolled over very **slowly**. The piece of apple stayed on top of her head.

"Sit," said Leeza.

Bella gently sat up.

"Okay, get it."

Bella flicked her head. The apple piece flew up into the air and landed in her mouth.

Kate giggled and clapped.

Lindie Lou looked up at Leeza. She wanted a piece of the apple.

"Is it okay if I give this to Lindie Lou?" asked Leeza. She was holding up a piece of apple.

"Sure," answered Kate. "Lindie Lou has never tasted an apple before."

"Here you go, Lindie Lou," said Leeza. "I don't expect you to put on the same show Bella did."

Leeza bent down and handed Lindie Lou a piece of apple. She sniffed it and took a bite.

The flavor was amazing. Lindie Lou had never tasted anything like it. The apple tasted a little sweet, a little sour, kind of juicy, and very crunchy. Lindie Lou chewed it up, then begged for more.

"She liked it," said Leeza.

"She sure did," replied Kate.

Leeza threw two pieces of apple into the air. Bella and Lindie Lou jumped up at the same time and caught their treats before they hit the floor.

"That was cool," said Kate.

"Apples are a big part of New York's history," said Leeza. "There are many apple trees growing in this state."

"Is that why New York City is called the **BIG APPLE**?" asked Kate.

"I think the name came from a legend," said Leeza. She brought a plate of apples over to the table and sat down. "When I was a little girl, my father told me the story."

"Do tell," said Kate.

"Let's see. . .," said Leeza. "Oh yes. Many years ago, a fleet of ships sailed across the Atlantic Ocean. They were coming from Europe to a place called the New World. These ships carried many things. They brought people, food, tools, and animals. Some of the people packed seeds to plant in their new gardens. One little boy loved apples, so he brought a handful of apple seeds.

"When the ships arrived, the people traveled across the land looking for an ideal place to live. The little boy followed his parents. Along the way, he planted all of his seeds but one. The seed he kept was the **largest** of them all."

Kate picked up a piece of apple and took a bite.

"The little boy's family found a great place to build their new home. Meanwhile, the boy looked for the perfect spot to plant his last apple seed. He chose an area where the soil was rich and there was plenty of sun."

Leeza gave the puppies another piece of apple.

"The boy planted his seed and watered it every day. Over many years, the seed grew into a big apple tree. Every year the boy picked RIPE RED APPLES from his tree. He proudly shared his apples with his family and friends."

Leeza took a bite of an apple.

"Legend says the apples on this tree are sweeter and juicier than any other apples on earth."

Hey, thought Lindie Lou. *I'd like to taste some of those apples.*

"As the years went by, the boy grew into a man. His name was Johnny. He kept taking care of his tree for the rest of his life. Johnny noticed the apples on this tree were growing bigger every year. Some of the apples grew even **bigger** than a grapefruit."

"Wow," said Kate.

Lindie Lou listened carefully.

"I've asked many people about the tree," said Leeza. "No one has seen it. But I understand the boy planted it right here on Manhattan Island."

"I wonder where," said Kate.

"There's more to the story," said Leeza. She held her finger up to her lips. "But it's a secret," she whispered.

Chapter 9

THE SECRET OF THE BIG APPLE

Kate slid to the edge of her chair.

"Can you tell me the secret?" she asked Leeza.

"I CAN'T tell you the secret,
but I CAN tell you what it's about."

"Okay," said Kate. She leaned closer to Leeza.

"If someone finds the tree, I understand it will reveal a secret so *amazing*, so *incredible*, and so *important*, it can change their life," said Leeza.

"Oh my gosh!" shouted Kate. She jumped up so fast her chair almost **tipped** over. "Let's go find the Big Apple Tree."

Leeza shook her head.

"The tree would be several hundred years old by now," said Leeza. "Apple trees don't live that long."

"Maybe someone planted seeds from the original tree," said Kate.

"It is possible," said Leeza. "But Tomas, Bella, and I have been all over this island, and we can't find it."

Kate sat down and sighed.

"Maybe it *is* just a legend."

Leeza nodded.

"Well, if you can't find the tree, I probably won't be able to find it either," said Kate. "Besides, Bryan and I are only staying for a few more days, and we have a lot of work to do on your new book."

"Agreed," said Leeza.

I'd like to look for the Big Apple Tree AND uncover its secret, thought Lindie Lou.

All of a sudden Lindie Lou could hardly wait to go outside. She jumped up and ran to the front door. Bella followed her.

"Maybe WE can find the Big Apple Tree," said Lindie Lou.

"I've looked before," said Bella. "But we can look some more."

"Then we're going on a New York City adventure," said Lindie Lou. "Arooo," she howled.

Bella howled, too.

Tomas and Bryan rushed into the kitchen.

"What is all the noise about?" asked Bryan.

"The pups are at the front door," said Tomas. "Looks like they'd like to go outside."

"I'm ready for our run," said Bryan.

"Me too," said Tomas. "Let's go together."

Chapter 10

I HAVE NEWS

Tomas, Bryan, Bella, and Lindie Lou took the elevator to the main floor. Tomas led them out of the building. They jogged over to the corner. Bella sat near the curb. Lindie Lou sat next to her.

"Bella's waiting for the signal light to change," said Tomas. "When it chirps, she knows it's safe to cross the street."

"You've trained her well," said Bryan. "Can you track her?"

Tomas held up Bella's tracking device. He pushed a button, and Bella's collar blinked. Bryan reached into his pocket. He held up Lindie Lou's tracking device. Bryan pushed a button, and Lindie Lou's collar blinked.

"Looks like their urban off-leash collars and tracking devices are working," said Tomas. "Bella has a lot of friends in the park. I'm sure they'll be okay on their own."

"Okay," said Bryan.

Tomas and Bryan unhooked their dogs' leashes.

The traffic light turned green, and chirped like a bird. Bella crossed the street. Lindie Lou followed. Tomas and Bryan crossed with them. They waved goodbye to the pups and jogged north toward a clear blue lake.

"Follow me," said Bella. "I'd like you to meet some of my friends."

It was a chilly November morning. Lindie Lou could feel the cold autumn wind against her face. People and pets were strolling through Central Park. Colorful autumn leaves floated down from the trees. The leaves reminded Lindie Lou of Saint Louis, where she was born. But today seemed much colder. Lindie Lou was glad she had a fluffy coat of fur to keep her warm.

"Over here," said Bella. She romped across the grass toward a row of evergreen bushes.

"Hey, Bella," came a voice from behind a bush. "I see you brought a friend."

"Her name is Lindie Lou," replied Bella. "Don't worry. She's cool."

A large, black-and-tan, short-haired dog came out from behind the bushes. Three smaller dogs followed. They walked over to Lindie Lou and sniffed her fur. Lindie Lou looked at Bella. She smiled and winked.

The large dog sat down in front of Lindie Lou.

"My name is Saul," he said. Saul raised his head with pride.

"I have news," said Bella.

Saul's eyes grew wider.

"Do tell," he said. Saul perked up his ears.

"This morning Lindie Lou heard my owner tell a story about an apple tree growing somewhere on this island. Legend says the apples on this tree are sweeter and juicier than any other apples on earth. Some of the apples are supposed to be even **bigger** than a grapefruit."

"Hmm," said Saul. "I've never seen this tree."

"My owner called it the Big Apple Tree. She also said this apple tree holds a secret so *amazing*, so *incredible*, and so *important*, it can change your life."

"Oh yeah?" replied Saul. "The only apple trees I've seen around here are crab apple trees." Saul looked around. "There's one." He was looking over the top of Lindie Lou's head.

Bella and Lindie Lou turned around.

A small tree with

short twisted

branches stood behind them. Most of its leaves were on the ground.

"Crab apples grow in the summer," said Saul. "They taste kinda **SOUR** and are about the size of a ping-pong ball."

One of the other dogs stepped forward. He had wiry, reddish-brown fur, short legs, and a **long,** thin body. His name was Brody.

"I've heard the legend of the Big Apple Tree," said Brody. All of the other dogs turned and listened. "I understand the apples on this tree grow all year round. This is why they grow bigger than other apples on other trees. I also heard the apples are so sweet, they taste like

Brody continued.

"I haven't seen the tree, but I'm told the legend is true, and the tree is real."

"Have either of you seen this tree?" asked Saul. The other dogs shook their heads. "Well, we have better things to do around here than look for a tree based on a legend," said Saul. He stood up, turned, and walked back toward the bushes. "See ya later."

Lindie Lou and Bella watched the dogs disappear behind the bushes.

"Well, I'd like to try to find a tree with apples so sweet they taste like candy," said Lindie Lou. She raised her nose and sniffed the air. "I think I smell apples." Lindie Lou sniffed again. "And I think I smell candy, too."

Lindie Lou jumped up and looked at Bella.

"Follow me,"

barked Lindie Lou.

Chapter 11

LOOKING FOR APPLES

Lindie Lou ran to the edge of Central Park. Bella followed her. They came to a busy street. Car pods zoomed by. Lindie Lou wondered when it would be safe to cross the street. She remembered Bella waited for a chirping sound before she crossed the street.

Lindie Lou saw the signal light change from red to green. Then she heard the chirping sound. All of the car pods stopped. When the path was clear, Lindie Lou crossed the street. Bella followed.

They walked for a long time until they came to a shopping area. Crowds of people were walking by. Many shoppers carried shopping bags. Some were sitting on benches. Others strolled by store windows. Lindie Lou looked up and saw bright neon billboards blinking above their heads.

"This place is called Times Square," said Bella. She looked around. "I don't think we'll find any apple trees around here. There are too many buildings."

Lindie Lou kept walking. She sniffed the air until she came to a brightly lit store window. She sat down and looked up.

"I don't see an apple tree," said Bella.

"It's a candy store," said Lindie Lou. "Take a look on the top shelf."

Bella looked up and saw a row of bright red candy apples.

"Your nose brought us here?" asked Bella.

"Yes," said Lindie Lou. "The apples up there are sweet, and they're covered with candy."

"But they're not on a tree, and they're not as big as a grapefruit," said Bella.

"I was hoping they would be," said Lindie Lou. She put her head down.

A lady walked out of the store with a little boy. She was holding his hand. In her other hand was a Hershey's candy apple. The lady stopped to give the little boy a bite. Lindie Lou and Bella walked over and wagged their tails.

"Sorry," said the lady. "Candy apples are much too sweet for puppies." She smiled, took the boy's hand, and walked away. The little boy looked back at Lindie Lou and Bella. His face was covered with **STICKY** chocolate and candy.

Darn, thought Lindie Lou. *I would have liked to take a bite of that candy apple.* She turned and looked around.

There was a GIANT WHITE APPLE painted on one of the shop's windows. It had a bite taken out of it. Lindie Lou knew she couldn't eat this apple because it was painted on the window. She looked for another clue.

Someone must know where the Big Apple Tree is growing, thought Lindie Lou. She looked around.

Down the street was a shop selling fruit and veggie juices. A man came out of the shop carrying a tray of fresh cut fruit, carrots, and some colorful drink samples. Lindie Lou and Bella walked over and sat by his feet. The man gave them a piece of a green apple. It tasted really sour. Lindie Lou wrinkled her nose and **shook** her head.

"Apples are good for you,"
said the man.
"They are full of fiber and vitamin C.
If you eat an apple every day,
they will keep you healthy.
And they're good for your teeth, too."

I just learned a helpful lesson about apples, thought Lindie Lou.

The man gave Lindie Lou and Bella another bite. It still tasted sour.

"I think you would prefer a sweet red apple," said the man. Lindie Lou licked her lips. He looked at Lindie Lou. "There's a bakery on this island called Petee's Pie Company," said the man. "The owner Petra makes the sweetest apple pies you'll ever taste." The man leaned closer to Lindie Lou. "During the week, she gives out free samples."

"Yum," barked Lindie Lou. "If Petra makes a lot of apple pies, she might be getting her apples from the Big Apple Tree."

"I know where Petee's Pie Company is," said Bella.

"You do?" asked Lindie Lou.

"Yes," said Bella.

"Follow me."

Chapter 12

THE SUBWAY

Lindie Lou followed Bella around a corner and down a steep stairway.

"Where are we going?" asked Lindie Lou.

"We're taking a subway train," said Bella. "Dogs ride for free."

Bella led Lindie Lou through a long tunnel under the street. Lindie Lou saw a train whiz by.

"I didn't know trains run underneath the city," said Lindie Lou.

"They run under the rivers, too," said Bella.

"Amazing," said Lindie Lou.

"Our train will be here soon."

"How do you know which one to take?" asked Lindie Lou.

"I can tell by the color," said Bella. "Today we're taking a red one." She looked at Lindie Lou. "When we get on the train, make sure to stay close to me. A lot of people ride the subway trains. I don't want you to get lost."

Lindie Lou nodded.

A few moments later, a red train slowed down and stopped in front of them. The doors slid open, and a crowd of people stepped off. More people RUSHED on. Bella and Lindie Lou followed them.

Lindie Lou liked being on a train. It moved very fast. Not as fast as an airplane, but this train moved along the track at a fast pace. Lights outside the window zoomed by. When the train made a turn, the wheels

squealed

along the tracks. Lindie Lou enjoyed the motion, the lights, and the sound.

"How do you know where to get off?" asked Lindie Lou.

"I travel on these trains all the time," said Bella. "Tomas showed me where to get on and get off. Each station looks different. We'll exit at a station with yellow flowers painted on the walls."

"You're a smart puppy," said Lindie Lou.

The train stopped many times. Groups of people stepped off the train. Others rushed on. When they arrived at a station with yellow flowers painted on the walls, Bella nudged Lindie Lou.

"It's time to get off," said Bella.

Lindie Lou followed Bella off the train and up a steep ramp. It took a minute for Lindie Lou's eyes to adjust to the daylight.

A giant ice-blue building stood in front of them. Lindie Lou had never seen

anything like it. The building was very tall. It reached up above the clouds. Birds soared around its windows.

"Wow," said Lindie Lou. "What a stunning building."

"It's called the One World Trade Center," said Bella.

Lindie Lou sat down and looked up at the building for a long time. She especially liked to watch the birds.

"There's another great building right around the corner," said Bella. "It's called the Oculus. It's shaped like a giant white bird."

"Let's go see it," said Lindie Lou.

Bella led Lindie Lou around the corner. In front of them stood the most amazing building Lindie Lou had ever seen.

"Wow," said Lindie Lou. "The Oculus does look like a giant white bird. I like its curved wings."

"There's a subway station underneath," said Bella. "And a shopping center called the Hub."

"Cool," said Lindie Lou. "It sure is beautiful. The Oculus reminds me of the birds I saw flying around the One World Trade Center."

Bella nodded, and then she looked down the street.

"Hey, Lindie Lou," said Bella. "Petee's Pie Company is very near. Come on. I'll show you the way."

"Okay," said Lindie Lou. She turned and followed Bella.

They walked for a few blocks until Lindie Lou smelled something really tasty. She ran past Bella and up to the front of Petee's Pie Company. Lindie Lou looked through the glass window. Several pies were on display.

A sign near the front door said, "Service Dogs ONLY."

"We're not allowed inside," said Bella.

"Only dogs who are trained to help people can enter."

Lindie Lou looked around.

"I have an idea," said Lindie Lou.

Chapter 13

SEARCHING FOR APPLES

Bella followed Lindie Lou down the alley. They were behind Petee's Pie Company. Lindie Lou saw a loading dock. She climbed up some wooden steps. At the top of the steps was a bunch of empty boxes with apples printed on them. Lindie Lou saw an open door. She headed toward the door.

"You're going inside?" asked Bella.

"I smell apple pie," said Lindie Lou. She walked through the open door.

Bella climbed up the steps. She walked over to the door. Bella sniffed around and then followed Lindie Lou inside.

Lindie Lou and Bella walked down a hallway. They saw more empty boxes. On the other end of the hall was a shiny metal door. Lindie Lou went over to the door. She gently pushed it open. Bella and Lindie Lou LOOKED inside.

Five people were working in a hot, steamy kitchen. They wore white hairnets and bright red aprons. The workers were so busy they didn't see

Lindie Lou and Bella sneak into the room. They hid behind a dusty bag of flour.

One of the workers threw a lump of pastry dough onto a stone table. He rolled the dough flat. Then he placed the dough into a pie pan. Another cook covered the dough with apple pieces and warm syrup. The next cook sprinkled brown sugar on top. Another cook slid the pie into a hot oven.

Two other workers stood next to a pile of apples. They picked them up and peeled them as fast as they could.

"It smells amazing in here," whispered Lindie Lou.

A young lady with short brown hair rushed into the kitchen. She was wearing a bright green apron. Red apples were painted on it. The name "Petra" was written in big white letters across the top of her apron.

"We just received an order for twenty-five apple pies," said Petra.

"The order must be ready by tomorrow morning." Petra looked around the room. "Do we have enough apples to fill the order?"

"Not for twenty-five pies," said one of the workers.

Petra folded her arms and looked at the ceiling. She was hoping for a miracle.

One of the cooks wiped his hands on his apron and walked over to Petra. His name was Tony.

"I think I can solve our problem," said Tony. "I was waiting for the right time to tell you about a local legend."

Everyone paused and listened.

"There is an apple tree growing somewhere on this island," said Tony. "Legend says the apples on this tree are the

biggest, sweetest, juiciest

apples on earth." Tony held his finger in the air. "Some people say the apples on this tree are even bigger than a grapefruit."

Everyone gasped.

Lindie Lou and Bella looked at each other and smiled.

"Do you know where to find this tree?" asked Petra.

"I know where to find the person who told me about the legend," said Tony. "She should know where it is."

Petra pointed to two other workers. "You two, please go with Tony. Find this tree and bring back as many apples as you can carry," said Petra.

Petra picked up three brown burlap bags and handed them to Tony. The three cooks removed their hairnets and aprons. Then they rushed toward the back door.

The cooks were in such a hurry, they didn't see Lindie Lou and Bella hiding behind the bag of flour. Tony pulled the door open, and the cooks ran out.

Lindie Lou
and Bella
followed them.

Chapter 14

APPLES

The three cooks ran into the streets of New York City. They headed west, then turned north. Lindie Lou and Bella followed them. Tony stopped to speak to a lady at a fruit stand. She pointed north. Tony thanked her and headed north.

The three cooks ran until they reached Union Square Green Market on East 17th Street. Tony rushed up to a lady behind one of the fruit stands.

Lindie Lou and Bella saw the woman shake her head from side to side.

Tony stopped at many other food stands. He spoke to a lot of people. Meanwhile, Tony told the other two cooks to buy as many apples as they

could carry. When Tony reached the end of the market, he talked to the owner at the last stand. She also shook her head.

The other two cooks hurried over to Tony with three bags full of apples. They picked them up, **flung** them over their shoulders, and headed back to Petee's Pie Company.

"Looks like Tony and his helpers have enough apples to make twenty-five pies," said Bella.

"Sure does," said Lindie Lou. "But they didn't find the Big Apple Tree."

Bella looked around the market. People were packing up and getting ready to leave.

"It's late," said Bella. "We better head home." She looked at Lindie Lou. "We can search for the **BIG APPLE TREE** again tomorrow."

Lindie Lou looked up at the sky. The sun was starting to set.

"Okay," said Lindie Lou.

They walked to the nearest subway station.

When they were almost home, they exited the subway and walked into Central Park.

Saul and his friends came out from behind the bushes.

"Hey, Bella," barked Saul. "Did you find the Big Apple Tree?"

"Maybe," barked Bella.

Lindie Lou looked shocked.

"Don't worry," whispered Bella to Lindie Lou. "This will be fun. I have a plan."

"Where is it?" asked Saul.

"Follow me," barked Bella.

Bella turned and started to run. Lindie Lou ran after her. Saul and the other dogs chased Bella and

Lindie Lou. When they reached the street, the traffic signal chirped.

"I've never seen them leave the park," barked Bella.

Bella and Lindie Lou ran across the street. Saul and his friends stopped at the signal light. They noticed the road was clear, so they ran across the street.

"Oh no!" barked Bella. "My plan didn't work!"

"I have a plan," said Lindie Lou. She ran past Bella and up the driveway of the Gray Stone Manor. Bella followed her. They ran past the doorman and up the steps. Lindie Lou stopped at the top of the steps.

"Why are we stopping?" asked Bella.

"If they didn't stop at the street, they won't stop here either," said Lindie Lou.

"What are we going to do?" barked Bella.

Saul and his friends ran around the corner. They were about to run up the steps when Lindie Lou looked at the dragons.

"Rharr," growled Lindie Lou.

Saul and his friends came to a screeching halt. They looked at the dragons.

"What are those creepy-looking things?" barked Saul.

"Dragons," growled Lindie Lou. "They protect this building and the people who live inside." Lindie Lou **growled** again.

Saul and his friends backed down the driveway. They turned, and ran away.

"Nice going," said Bella. "I'm glad you had a plan."

"Me too," replied Lindie Lou. She looked up at the dragons, smiled, and walked into the building.

The doorman shook his head and smiled.

Bella and Lindie Lou walked down the hallway to the round room with the green glass ceiling. Gundula was sitting at her desk.

"She has treats," whispered Bella.

They sat down next to Gundula.

Gundula reached into her desk drawer and pulled out two **treats**. She gave one to each of them.

She's not so scary after all, thought Lindie Lou.

When Bella and Lindie Lou finished eating their treats, Gundula pushed a button on her desk.

"The elevator awaits you," said Gundula.

Bella stood up and walked toward the elevator. Lindie Lou looked at Gundula.

"I have a message for you," whispered Gundula.

Lindie Lou tipped her head, stood up, and followed Bella.

"Did you hear what Gundula said?"

"No," said Bella. "I didn't hear anything." She kept walking. "It's been a long day. Let's go upstairs. I'm THIRSTY."

"Me too," said Lindie Lou.

Lindie Lou looked over her shoulder at Gundula.

Lindie Lou saw Gundula **wink**.

Chapter 15

A MESSAGE

The next morning Leeza added fresh sliced apples to Bella and Lindie Lou's food. Lindie Lou loved the taste of apples. She especially liked their **crunchy** texture. After breakfast, Lindie Lou walked over to the front door and sat down.

"What's the rush?" asked Bella.

"I think Gundula might have a message for me. Maybe it's a clue about where we can find the Big Apple Tree," said Lindie Lou.

"I'm beginning to think the Big Apple Tree is just a legend," said Bella. She lay down and rested her chin on her paw.

"Well, I'd like to look for the tree one more day," barked Lindie Lou.

Kate heard Lindie Lou bark.

"Would you like to go outside?"

Lindie Lou **looked** up at Kate. Then she looked at the door.

"I'll take her with me," replied Bryan. "I'm ready to go for a run. Tomas had to go into work early today."

"Okay," said Kate.

Lindie Lou followed Bryan out of the apartment. They went down the elevator and walked into the round room with the green glass ceiling. Gundula was sitting at her desk.

Lindie Lou walked over and sat down next to Gundula.

"I guess she'd rather visit with you than go for a run," said Bryan.

"I'd love some company," replied Gundula.

Bryan smiled and left the room.

Gundula turned and looked at Lindie Lou.

"I have a message for you, Lindie Lou," Gundula said softly.

Lindie Lou's **eyes widened**.

Gundula gave Lindie Lou a warm smile. She stood up, walked over to Lindie Lou, and sat down next to her.

"Did you see the painting of me with a puppy on the eighth floor?"

Lindie Lou nodded.

"When I was younger, I had a puppy who looked just like you." Gundula reached over and petted Lindie Lou. "My puppy loved an adventure. I think you do, too, Lindie Lou."

Lindie Lou looked up at Gundula.

"You're looking for the Big Apple Tree, aren't you?"

Lindie Lou nodded again.

Gundula held out her hand. Lindie Lou lifted her paw and placed it in Gundula's hand.

"New York is a very **big** city," said Gundula. "It's also a magical city."

Lindie Lou tipped her head.

"If you wish to find the Big Apple Tree and uncover its secret, you will need some help."

Gundula looked around the room. She wanted to be sure they were alone.

"To help you find the tree, I'll give you some clues."

Gundula gently squeezed Lindie Lou's paw.

"Walk to the north end of Central Park. You will find a dirt path heading east. Follow the path until you see an

old stone staircase.

Climb the stairs to the top where you will find a narrow trail. Follow this trail up to the top of the hill."

Gundula looked deep into Lindie Lou's eyes.

"The answer to the Big Apple Tree will be waiting for you at the top of the hill."

Lindie Lou **gasped**.

Gundula let go of Lindie Lou's paw. She stood up and went over to her desk.

Lindie Lou walked toward the door. Just before she left, she looked back at Gundula. She was waving.

"Good luck, my friend," said Gundula.

Lindie Lou **barked** twice, and then she ran outside.

Chapter 16

WHICH WAY?

I must remember what Gundula told me, thought Lindie Lou. *She said to go north until I find a dirt path, then east, then look for an old stone staircase. Go up the stairs to a narrow dirt trail. This trail will lead me to the top of a hill.*

Lindie Lou crossed the street, entered Central Park, and looked around. *Which way is north?* she wondered.

Saul appeared from behind a bush.

"What are you doing in the park so early?" asked Saul.

Lindie Lou shuddered and backed up.

"Don't worry. I won't harm you," said Saul. He walked over to Lindie Lou. "You're still looking for the Big Apple Tree, aren't you?"

Lindie Lou looked around.

"I was wondering which way north is," Lindie Lou said quietly.

"Why do you want to know?" asked Saul. He walked in a slow circle around Lindie Lou.

"I was told to go to the north end of the park and then go east."

"Is the Big Apple Tree over there?" asked Saul.

"I'm not sure," said Lindie Lou. "But I'd like to find out."

"If I tell you which way north and east are, will you tell me what you find?"

"Yes," said Lindie Lou.

"Then we're friends?" asked Saul.

"**Friends**," repeated Lindie Lou.

Saul smiled, and then he looked up toward the sun.

Lindie Lou looked up, too.

"Every morning the sun rises in the east," said Saul. He sat down, lifted his

right paw, and pointed in the direction of the sun. Lindie Lou did the same.

"Every evening the sun sets in the west," said Saul. He set his right paw down, lifted his left paw, and pointed in the other direction.

Lindie Lou did the same.

"If your right paw faces east, and your left paw faces west, then your nose will be pointing north, and your tail will be pointing south."

Lindie Lou looked at her paws.

"I get it," said Lindie Lou. She looked at Saul. "Thank you."

"I hope you find the Big Apple Tree, Lindie Lou," said Saul.

"Me too," said Lindie Lou.

Lindie Lou turned and *ran* in the direction of her nose. Saul smiled and walked back behind the bushes.

When Lindie Lou reached the north end of the park, she sat down and

pointed her right paw toward the morning sun. She looked past her paw and found a dirt path. Lindie Lou ran up the path toward the east. It wasn't long before she found the old stone staircase leading up to a narrow dirt trail. The trail led up the side of a hill.

Wow, thought Lindie Lou. *Gundula gave me great directions so far. I hope the Big Apple Tree is up here.*

Lindie Lou followed the narrow dirt trail until she reached the top of the hill.

Chapter 17

WHAT'S UP HERE?

Lindie Lou walked around on top of the hill. She could hear

children playing

in the distance. Lindie Lou walked past a row of tall bushes. Behind the bushes was an old stone building. It reminded her of a fort she had seen in one of Kate's drawings. She walked around

the outside of the old stone building until she found the entrance. A brick staircase led her up to a large metal gate. She looked through the gate.

The old stone building didn't have a roof. It had rotted away years ago. The sun's rays shined down on the dry dirt floor. In the middle of the fort, Lindie Lou saw an American flag on top of a flagpole. It waved gently in the wind.

This place must have been important to someone a very long time ago, thought Lindie Lou. She looked around. A few twisted vines clung to the walls of the fort.

I don't see any apple trees in here, thought Lindie Lou. She sighed, turned, and climbed down the steps of the old stone fort.

Lindie Lou walked around the top of the hill, looking for the Big Apple Tree. In front of her was a giant boulder. She jumped up to get a better look. She could see a lot better from up here.

Lindie Lou looked to the left. . . no apple tree. She looked to the right. . . still no apple tree. She walked toward the edge of the boulder and looked down over New York City. It was a beautiful sunny autumn day. It seemed a bit warmer than the day before. Colorful trees framed her view of the buildings in the distance.

Then Lindie Lou noticed something move on the rocky ledge below her. She saw an old man sitting on a flat rock.

"Hey," barked Lindie Lou.

The man turned around and looked up at her.

"Hi," said the man. "You must be Lindie Lou."

Lindie Lou's mouth dropped open.

"How did you know my name?"

The old man held up his arm.

Lindie Lou saw a device on his wrist. It looked just like the one Gundula wore.

"Gundula told me."

"How do I know I can trust you?" asked Lindie Lou.

The man took a piece of paper out of his pocket and unfolded it. "Here is a picture of me with Gundula." He held it up so Lindie Lou could see it.

I'm glad Kate and Bryan taught me how to ask for proof before I trust a stranger.

"My name is Kris. I've been Gundula's friend since we were kids. Why don't you come and join me?"

Lindie Lou followed a path down to the spot where Kris was sitting.

He was a chubby old fellow, with long *wavy* hair and a BUSHY beard. His blue eyes twinkled, and his smile was friendly.

"Gundula told me I'd find the Big Apple Tree up here," said Lindie Lou.

"Oh, did she?" asked Kris. He chuckled. Then he reached over and petted Lindie Lou on the head. "Did you find it?"

"No," answered Lindie Lou. She sat down. "I've looked everywhere on this hill, and I can't find it."

"What if I told you the tree is invisible?" said Kris.

Lindie Lou looked up at him.

"Is that why no one can find it?" asked Lindie Lou.

Kris nodded.

"Wait a minute," said Lindie Lou. "How can the Big Apple Tree bear the biggest, sweetest, juiciest apples on earth if it's invisible?"

Kris raised his finger.

"Things that are invisible to many,

may be visible to some.

All you have to do

is know what to look for."

Lindie Lou thought for a moment.

"I'd like to know what to look for," said Lindie Lou.

"If you're willing to

listen carefully and be open-minded,

I can help you see the Big Apple Tree," said Kris.

Hmm. . . thought Lindie Lou. *I had to be open-minded when Saul explained north, south, east, and west to me.*

Lindie Lou stood up and looked at Kris.

"I'm ready," barked Lindie Lou.

"Okay," said Kris. He turned his head and looked over New York City.

"Take a look out there," said Kris.

"The Big Apple Tree is right in front of you."

Chapter 18

CLOSE YOUR EYES

Lindie Lou looked over New York City. Then she looked up at Kris.

"I don't see any apple trees," said Lindie Lou.

"Close your eyes," said Kris.

Lindie Lou closed her eyes.

"The legend says. . . there is a tree," said Kris.

Lindie Lou nodded.

"The apples on this tree are **bigger**, sweeter, and juicier than any other apples on earth."

Lindie Lou nodded again and licked her lips.

"Some people say the apples on this tree are even bigger than a grapefruit."

"Exactly," barked Lindie Lou. She stood up on her hind legs and howled.

"Be careful," said Kris. He gently held on to Lindie Lou.

Lindie Lou opened her eyes and looked down. The flat rock they were on was way up above the trees.

Kris lifted Lindie Lou onto his lap. He tilted his head and said slowly,

"If you act without thinking,
you might get into trouble.
If you think before you act,
you will be much safer."

Lindie Lou looked up at Kris. "Thank you. I'll try to be more careful from now on."

Kris smiled, looked down, and pointed to a trail.

"Do you see that trail over there?" asked Kris.

"Yes," answered Lindie Lou.

"It winds down around the hill."

"I see," said Lindie Lou.

"Now close your eyes again," said Kris.

Lindie Lou closed her eyes.

"Imagine what it would be like if this hill was a giant tree trunk."

"I can imagine it," said Lindie Lou.

"Good," said Kris. "Now **imagine** large branches growing out of the trunk of this tree."

Lindie Lou nodded.

"The branches are very long. Some grow around this hill until they reach the city."

Lindie Lou nodded again.

"The branches keep growing. Some turn into the streets of New York City."

"I see it," said Lindie Lou.

"Okay," said Kris. "Now **imagine** at the end of the branches are thousands of leaves."

Lindie Lou nodded.

"Those leaves are the people of New York City."

Lindie Lou gasped. "Then the **APPLES** must be their heads," barked Lindie Lou.

"Correct," said Kris.

Lindie Lou kept her eyes closed. She could **finally** see the Big Apple Tree. It was more amazing than she ever imagined. The tree was this entire hill, the trails, the streets of New York, and even the people.

New York City **was** the Big Apple Tree.

"The legend of the Big Apple Tree is even cooler than I ever imagined," said Lindie Lou.

"You can open your eyes now," said Kris.

Chapter 19

A WHOLE NEW CITY

Lindie Lou opened her eyes and looked out over New York City. It was as if she was seeing it for the first time. She looked at the buildings. She looked down at the car pods driving by. She could hear children playing and see people walking everywhere.

"New York City is **alive**. Just like a tree is **alive**," said Lindie Lou.

"Exactly," replied Kris. "The Big Apple Tree was around you all the time.

All you had to do was know where to **LOOK** for it."

Kris put his arm around Lindie Lou. She smiled up at him. He had given her a special gift, and for this she was truly grateful.

Lindie Lou sat on top of the hill with Kris for the rest of the day. He told her what he liked about living in New York City. He pointed out the Empire State Building and told her about the shows at Radio City Music Hall. Kris also told Lindie Lou the history of Ellis Island. Then he asked her what she liked about the city.

Lindie Lou told Kris about all of the special people she had met. She liked riding on subway trains and seeing the Oculus.

"Without all of my new friends' help, I never would have found this hill. I never would have met you. I never would have found the Big Apple Tree."

Kris smiled and gave Lindie Lou a friendly hug.

"New York City is like a giant puzzle,"

said Lindie Lou. "A magical puzzle. And now all of the pieces seem to fit."

"So true," said Kris.

Lindie Lou suddenly felt peaceful up on the hill, in Central Park, with Kris. She had found the Big Apple Tree, and she was smiling.

"Tell me more about you and your friends," said Lindie Lou.

"I'm retired," said Kris. "A lot of my friends are retired, too. Which means we don't have to work. But it doesn't mean we sit around doing nothing. Sometimes I like to paint. Often my friends and I spend our day keeping the

Big Apple clean and granting people's wishes."

"You granted my wish today," said Lindie Lou.

Kris smiled at Lindie Lou. He reached in his pocket and pulled out a plastic bag.

"By picking up trash like this, not only do we keep the city clean, we save animals who may get hurt if they chew on things like this."

"Nice," said Lindie Lou. "Do you and your friends call New York City the Big Apple?"

"We sure do," replied Kris.

"I'm going to call it the Big Apple," said Lindie Lou.

"Great idea," replied Kris.

Lindie Lou realized she wanted to share the legend of the Big Apple Tree with others.

"Is it okay if I tell my friends about the Big Apple Tree?" asked Lindie Lou.

"I think you should," replied Kris. "I wish everybody knew about the tree. But let me warn you. . ." Kris looked at Lindie Lou. "Not everyone will see things as clearly as you do."

Lindie Lou stood up.

"I'd like to try," said Lindie Lou. "Thank you for helping me find the Big Apple Tree. I hope I see you again."

"I hope so, too," said Kris.

Lindie Lou turned and ran down the hill.

Chapter 20

I CAN'T WAIT

"I'm so excited!" barked Lindie Lou. She did a little *dance*. "I found the Big Apple Tree," sang Lindie Lou. She jumped up in the air and flipped over. Then Lindie Lou continued running through the park.

When she came to the exit near Tomas and Leeza's house, Saul appeared.

"Where are you going in such a hurry?" asked Saul. "I've been waiting for you."

Lindie Lou came to a

SCREECHING HALT.

"I'm on my way to Bella's house," said Lindie Lou.

"Hey, my friend. Did you find the Big Apple Tree?" asked Saul.

"Well. . .," said Lindie Lou. "Actually, I did. But it's not what you think."

"Do tell," said Saul. He walked around Lindie Lou. "Remember your promise?"

Lindie Lou sat down.

"Okay," said Lindie Lou. "The Big Apple Tree isn't like the trees in this park." She looked around. "It's actually all of New York City."

"Oh really?" said Saul. "Tell me more."

Lindie Lou told Saul about meeting Kris on top of the hill. She told him Kris said the tree was invisible, unless you know what to **LOOK** for.

"Everyone and everything in New York City is part of the Big Apple Tree," explained Lindie Lou.

"Then how can I taste the sweetest, juiciest apples on earth?" asked Saul.

"You taste them every day," answered Lindie Lou. "The sweetest part of New York City is. . . this park. The place where you come every day to meet your friends and play."

"And the juiciest part?" asked Saul.

"It's the water you drink, the air you breathe, and the treats people give you."

Saul thought about what Lindie Lou

was telling him. He walked around her one more time.

"Is this the legend of the Big Apple Tree?" asked Saul.

"Yes," replied Lindie Lou. "Can you see it?"

Saul looked around the park.

"No, I can't." He shook his head.

"Then follow me," said Lindie Lou.

She walked toward the west exit of Central Park. On the sidewalk was a mosaic picture of a sun. Seven letters were written in the middle of the sun.

"Can you read?" asked Lindie Lou.

"Of course I can," barked Saul.

"Then read this," said Lindie Lou.

"Imagine," said Saul. He stared at the word. Then he lifted his head and looked around the park.

"I get it," said Saul. He smiled.

Lindie Lou jumped up and spun in a circle.

"I'm glad you can see the Big Apple Tree," said Lindie Lou. She looked at Saul and then at the exit.

"I can't wait to tell Bella!" barked Lindie Lou. She said goodbye to Saul and ran toward the Gray Stone Manor.

"Thank you, my friend," called Saul. "I'm glad we met. You have given me an amazing gift."

Chapter 21

IT MUST BE MAGIC

Lindie Lou ran up the steps of the Gray Stone Manor. She ran down the hallway and into the room with the green glass ceiling. She stopped at Gundula's desk.

"Thank you for telling me where to find the Big Apple Tree," said Lindie Lou.

"Then you met Kris and you now know. . .

Things that are invisible to many, may be visible to some?"

"Yes," replied Lindie Lou. "And I can't wait to tell Bella about the tree."

"Then the elevator awaits you," said Gundula. She reached over and pushed the button on her desk.

Lindie Lou ran into the elevator, rode up to the eighth floor, and ran down the hall. The apartment door was open. Bella was waiting by the door.

"Where have you been?" asked Bella. "I went to the park to look for you, but I couldn't find you."

"Did you talk to Saul?"

"No, he wasn't in the park when I was there," replied Bella.

Lindie Lou did a flip and landed on her back. She was grinning.

"You found the Big Apple Tree, didn't you?" asked Bella.

Lindie Lou nodded.

"Where is it?" asked Bella.

Lindie Lou rolled over and walked into the apartment. She jumped up on the bench near the window and sat down. Bella jumped up and sat next to her.

"Look out there," said Lindie Lou.

Bella looked out the window.

Lindie Lou told Bella about how Gundula gave her directions to go to the north side of Central Park. She told her about following a path up a hill and finding a fort.

"You must have been at the Blockhouse," said Bella.

"You know it?" asked Lindie Lou.

"Yes," answered Bella. "I've been there a few times, but I didn't see any apple trees up there."

Lindie Lou told Bella she had met a man up there named Kris. He knew about the Big Apple Tree. Then she told Bella why all of New York City is the Big Apple Tree.

"No wonder I couldn't find it," said Bella. "The Big Apple Tree is so much bigger than I imagined."

Lindie Lou nodded.

"Hey, wait a minute," said Bella.

"You TALKED to Gundula and you TALKED to Kris?"

"I did," replied Lindie Lou.

"Animals can't talk to humans."

"I never have before," said Lindie Lou.

"It must be magic," said Bella.

"Big City Magic," barked Lindie Lou.

They looked at each other. Then they looked at New York City.

"Hey, wait a minute," said Bella. "What about the secret?"

"Oh my gosh!" said Lindie Lou. "I was so excited about finding the Big Apple Tree, I forgot about the secret."

"What was it about?" asked Bella. She scratched her ear.

"I remember," said Lindie Lou. "Leeza said if you find the tree, it will reveal a secret so *amazing*, so *incredible*, and so *important*, it can change your life."

"But the Big Apple Tree is the entire city," said Bella.

"Then the city must reveal its secret to us," said Lindie Lou.

Bella and Lindie Lou looked at the city one more time. They watched the light of the sun disappear from the park.

Chapter 22

COULD IT BE?

The next morning Lindie Lou awoke to the sound of **LOUD** noises. It sounded like a lot of people clapping and cheering. She sat up, stretched out her huge paws, and walked into the living room.

Tomas, Leeza, Bryan, Kate, and Bella were sitting on the bench near the window.

"Look at the size of those balloons," said Leeza.

Bella **barked**. Kate clapped her hands. Lindie Lou jumped up on the bench and squeezed in between Kate and Bella.

"What's going on?" barked Lindie Lou.

"It's a parade," **howled** Bella.

A giant balloon floated by their window. It looked like a young boy. He had tiny black eyes and a big round head. He was holding a bright red book.

Lindie Lou **barked**.

"It's not a real boy," said Bella. "It's a balloon."

Lindie Lou looked again. Another balloon floated by. This one looked like a dog. The dog was sitting on top of a doghouse. Lindie Lou looked closer. The dog had a yellow bird sitting on top of his head.

Lindie Lou **barked** again.

"No more barking," said Bryan. He held up his finger and shook his head.

Lindie Lou looked out of the window again. She could hear a band playing. The song they played came from horns, drums, and bells. It reminded her of when she was in Des Moines at the Harvest Parade. People outside were clapping and singing.

Behind the band was a float with a **huge** red sleigh. It was being pulled by eight reindeer. In the front seat was a girl dressed in a green outfit. She looked like an elf.

Then Lindie Lou saw someone else in the sleigh.

Could it be? wondered Lindie Lou.

She looked very carefully.

Sure enough! It was Kris!

Kris was sitting in the back seat. He was wearing a red velvet coat with white trim. There was a giant bag of presents behind him. Kris was smiling and waving to the crowd.

"It's Kris," **barked** Lindie Lou.

"The man you met in the park, is in the parade?" asked Bella.

"Yes," **barked** Lindie Lou.

"Lindie Lou," scolded Kate. "We asked you not to bark." She lifted Lindie Lou up and set her on the floor.

Lindie Lou turned and **ran** toward the front door. Bella jumped down and followed her.

"This time I'm coming with you," said Bella. She pushed the door open, and the two pups ran down the hall.

When they reached the main floor, Bella and Lindie Lou ran past Gundula. She stood up and followed them to the door. Soon they were all out on the street.

The float Kris was on had passed by the Gray Stone Manor and was heading down the street.

"There it is," barked Bella.

"Wow, these floats are much bigger than they looked from upstairs."

Lindie Lou turned and ran as fast as she could. Bella was right behind her. When they caught up with the float, Lindie Lou took a

giant leap

and landed on one of the reindeer's big front hooves. Then she climbed up on its back.

Kris was watching Lindie Lou.

"Ho, ho, ho," called Kris.

"**Arf**, **arf**, **arf**," barked Lindie Lou.

Bella followed the float as it moved down the street.

"Look at that cute little puppy sitting on the back of one of the reindeer!" yelled a little boy from the crowd.

Everyone laughed

and cheered.

Chapter 23

IT'S THANKSGIVING DAY

"Ho, ho, ho," sang Kris. He was holding his belly. "Well, Lindie Lou, if you can get this far, you might as well come and sit next to me."

Lindie Lou crouched down and jumped up into the air. She landed on the head of another reindeer. Then she raised up her **huge** front paws and tried to jump on its back. Lindie Lou landed safely, but at the same time, the float was turning a corner. Lindie Lou's weight

shifted, and she started sliding off the reindeer. She quickly grabbed onto a string of jingle bells hanging around the reindeer's neck.

The elf in the green outfit reached down and grabbed Lindie Lou by the scruff of her neck.

"Where do you think you're going?" asked the elf. She held Lindie Lou up to her face and looked into her eyes.

"Maria," called Kris. "Thanks for rescuing Lindie Lou. She's a friend of mine."

Lindie Lou licked Maria on the nose.

"Please pass her to me."

"Okay," said Maria. "Here you go."

Maria handed Lindie Lou to Kris. He held her with both hands. They rubbed noses.

The crowd clapped and cheered. Kris held Lindie Lou up and showed her to everyone. They cheered some more.

"You'd better sit here," said Kris. He sat Lindie Lou down next to him. "Now you stay put," said Kris.

Lindie Lou nodded. Kris turned and waved at the crowd.

Lindie Lou looked at all of the people. There were thousands of happy faces along the parade route.

"Why are we in a parade?" asked Lindie Lou.

"Today is Thanksgiving Day," replied Kris. "This is the day everyone celebrates a successful harvest. We eat a special meal on this day. Before the meal, everyone gives thanks for all the good things that happened during the year. But, right now, it's time to celebrate."

Kris pointed to a few of his friends in the crowd. He stood up and waved.

"This parade is called the Macy's Thanksgiving Day Parade!" shouted Kris. "This is New York City's biggest parade of the year." He sat down next to Lindie

Lou. "This float we're on represents the beginning of the holiday season."

"Happy Thanksgiving Day!" howled Lindie Lou.

"Ho, ho, ho," sang Kris. He reached behind him and pulled out a red hat from his giant bag of gifts. It looked just like the one Kris was wearing. Kris placed it on Lindie Lou's head.

"**Woof**, **woof**, **woof**," barked Lindie Lou.

"Ho, ho, ho," replied Kris.

So THIS is Thanksgiving Day, thought Lindie Lou. *It sure is a lot of fun.* She looked at the crowd. *I wonder what I have to be thankful for,* thought Lindie Lou.

Chapter 24

I'M THANKFUL

Lindie Lou saw Bella running along the street next to the float.

"Can my friend join us?" asked Lindie Lou.

Kris looked down at Bella.

"Of course," replied Kris. "Maria, can you help Lindie Lou's friend up onto the float?"

Maria reached out her arms. Bella climbed up the side of the float. Maria scooped her up and set her on the seat next to her.

"Woo-hoo!" howled Bella. "You have a nice view of the crowd from up here."

"There's my dad, Jose, and my brother, Miguel," said Maria. She stood up and waved. "They came all the way from Puerto Rico to see me and this parade!"

"Ya-hoo-ee!" yelled Lindie Lou. She'd learned this word from Kate's cousin, Ronda. They had visited her last month during their harvest time.

The float turned the corner. Kris put his arm around Lindie Lou.

I have a lot to be thankful for, thought Lindie Lou. *I'm thankful for my owners, Kate and Bryan, for bringing* me on so many amazing adventures. I'm thankful for Joe and Sherry, who raised me. I'm thankful for my brothers and sisters, whom I miss a lot. I'm thankful for my stuffed animal friends Coco, Evy, and Manny. They are at home waiting to hear all about my adventures.

I'm also thankful for my new friends Tomas, Leeza, and Bella. They introduced me to this amazing city.

I'm thankful for Gundula, who is very wise and who guided me to Kris. And I'm thankful for my newest friend Maria for helping Bella and me get on this amazing float.

Lindie Lou looked up at Kris.

I am especially thankful for Kris, for helping me find the Big Apple Tree.

Then Lindie Lou looked at the thousands of people lining the streets of New York City. Some were holding babies, some were holding hands, and all of them were smiling and waving.

I am also thankful for being a part of this amazing Thanksgiving Day parade and making so many new friends.

"Ho, ho, ho," sang Kris again.

"**Arf, arf, arf**," barked Lindie Lou.

Bella howled.

Maria laughed. She turned to Kris.

"Where did you find such sweet puppies?" she asked.

"Lindie Lou found me in Central Park," replied Kris. He looked at Lindie Lou and winked.

The float continued to move down the street. Lindie Lou looked around and saw even more new faces.

"Hey, Lindie Lou," said Bella. "Look over there. It's the dogs from Central Park."

Lindie Lou saw Saul, Brody, and the other two dogs, Moe & Mika. They were with their owners. Bella and Lindie Lou **barked.**

They all barked back.

Lindie Lou looked down the street. She spotted the lady and her son from the candy store. The little boy saw Lindie Lou and Bella. He jumped up and down and ***waved***. Then Lindie Lou saw Tony and the cooks from Petee's Pie Company. Tony was holding a little girl's hand. Petra was standing with them. They were **waving**.

Lindie Lou sat up on her hind legs and looked over the crowd.

"Do you see someone you know?" asked Kris.

"I see many people I know," barked Lindie Lou.

Suddenly Lindie Lou realized exactly what she was seeing. She'd been in New York City for only two days and look at all the friends she had made.

Lindie Lou

gasped.

Chapter 25

A GREAT GIFT

Lindie Lou looked at the crowd.

Imagine if I were here for a week, a month, or even a year!

Lindie Lou smiled.

I would meet even more people and have even more friends!

Could it be? thought Lindie Lou. *Could the secret of the Big Apple be the fact that this city has so many people living in it that it is easier to make friends? Wait a minute.* Lindie

Lou looked around. *I think I've just uncovered the secret of the Big Apple!*

The secret is

friendship.

Lindie Lou's **eyes widened**. She looked at the crowd again.

Oh my gosh! thought Lindie Lou. *My friends are so amazing, so incredible, and so important, they HAVE changed my life.*

The parade continued down Central Park West to 59th Street. Then it moved eastward on 6th Avenue, the

route headed south again toward 34th Street, then west. It ended at Herald Square, right in front of Macy's department store.

Hundreds of children were waiting in front of Macy's. They chanted,

"Santa, Santa, Santa."

Kris waved to them. The sleigh slowed down, and Maria jumped off. Santa tossed her a bag of gifts. Maria handed them to the children.

Lindie Lou looked up at Kris.

"Why do they call you Santa?"

"Santa is my nick-name," said Kris. "Santa brings joy, hope, and gifts to everyone who believes in him."

"You've given me a great gift," said Lindie Lou.

"I have?"

"Yes," answered Lindie Lou. "You've given me your friendship."

Santa reached over, picked up Lindie Lou, and placed her on his lap.

"You're a very wise puppy," said Santa. "You've just uncovered the secret of the Big Apple."

Lindie Lou looked up at Santa. He was smiling and nodding. The float slowed down and stopped.

"Time to go," said Bella. "There's a Thanksgiving meal waiting for us at home."

Lindie Lou and Bella thanked Santa and Maria for the most amazing day of their lives. Then they jumped off the float and ran back toward Bella's house.

"Do you realize what just happened?" asked Lindie Lou.

"Yes," replied Bella. "We went TO a parade and ended up IN the parade."

"We did," replied Lindie Lou. "But something even more *amazing* happened when we were in the parade."

"What?" asked Bella.

"I uncovered the SECRET of the Big Apple."

Bella stopped and looked at Lindie Lou.

"You did? Wait a minute. Isn't the secret of the Big Apple the CITY of New York and everyone in it?"

"That's the LEGEND. New York City is the tree. The people in it are the leaves and the apples," replied Lindie Lou.

"But the SECRET is even bigger."

"It is?"

"Yes," replied Lindie Lou. "The SECRET is what you do in the Big City with everyone in it."

Bella scratched her head.

"And what exactly do you do?"

"Make friends,"

barked Lindie Lou.

Bella's mouth dropped open. She looked at Lindie Lou. Then she looked around the city as if she was seeing it for the very first time.

"The SECRET of the Big Apple is *amazing*," replied Bella.

On the way home, Bella and Lindie Lou talked about all of their friends. They also talked about how their friends had changed their lives.

"I'm glad you came to New York City," said Bella. "You've made me realize how

important my friends are

and how

amazing New York City is."

"This city is very big and very magical," replied Lindie Lou. "If you want, you can make friends everywhere. They can be inside the buildings, on the streets, or in the parks."

"They can be in the markets, on a subway train, and even on the Thanksgiving Day parade route," said Bella.

"Exactly," replied Lindie Lou. "All you have to do is want to make friends and be a friend in return."

"Thanks for being my friend," said Bella. She smiled and **bumped** Lindie Lou. Lindie Lou **bumped** her back.

"We're almost home," said Bella. "Let's go get some

Thanksgiving Day

."

Chapter 26

THE PIECE OF PAPER

The next morning Lindie Lou and Bella watched Kate and Bryan pack.

"Do you really have to leave?" asked Bella.

"I guess so," replied Lindie Lou. She put her head down. Then she looked at the door.

"Hey, Bella, let's go on one more adventure," said Lindie Lou.

"Seriously?" barked Bella.

Lindie Lou nodded. She ran to the front door,

pushed it open, and **ran**

out of the apartment. Bella followed her down the hall.

"Hey, look," said Bella.

Lindie Lou looked up at the wall. One of the paintings had been replaced. The new one had Gundula sitting at her desk. Lindie Lou was sitting on her lap.

"That's you and Gundula," said Bella.

"Oh, wow, it sure is,"

said Lindie Lou.

They walked over to the elevator. Lindie Lou sat down in front of the elevator door. Bella sat next to her.

"It won't open unless someone knows we're here," said Bella.

"I know," replied Lindie Lou.

A minute later, the door opened.

"Did Gundula open it?"

"I think so," said Lindie Lou.

Bella followed Lindie Lou into the elevator. It took them down to the main floor. They ran down the hall and into the room with the green glass ceiling.

Gundula was sitting at her desk. Lindie Lou went over and jumped up on one of the chairs in front of Gundula's desk. Bella jumped up on the other chair.

Lindie Lou saw Gundula write something on a piece of paper.

"I thought you said she talked to you," said Bella to Lindie Lou.

"She did," replied Lindie Lou.

"Then why isn't she talking to you now?" asked Bella.

"Maybe she doesn't have anything to say," answered Lindie Lou.

Bella scratched her head.

"What about the painting? Doesn't she want to tell you who painted it?" asked Bella.

"I guess not," said Lindie Lou.

They kept waiting for Gundula to speak. Gundula continued writing on the piece of paper. Lindie Lou jumped down from the chair and walked around the desk. Gundula smiled, reached down, and petted her on the top of her head.

"She still isn't talking," said Bella. She tipped her head. "Maybe you just imagined her talking to you."

"Gundula DID talk to me," **barked** Lindie Lou. "She's the one who told me where to find the **BIG APPLE TREE**."

Gundula put down her pen and held up the piece of paper. It said. . .

Believe.

Bella gasped.

"Did you see what she wrote?" asked Bella. "It says, Believe."

"Then believe," said Lindie Lou.

Gundula picked up Lindie Lou and set her on her lap.

"Do you know who painted the new painting up on the eighth floor?"

"Who?" asked Lindie Lou.

"My friend Kris," said Gundula. "He's your friend now, too."

Lindie Lou nodded.

"I'll never forget you, Lindie Lou," said Gundula. She gave her a hug.

"I'll never forget you either," said Lindie Lou. "Thank you for being my friend." She licked Gundula's chin.

Gundula squeezed Lindie Lou, again, and then she looked over and winked at Bella.

"She just talked to you," barked Bella.

Lindie Lou looked at Bella.

"Now do you believe?" asked Lindie Lou.

Chapter 27

WHERE WILL YOU GO NEXT?

The elevator doors opened on the main floor. Tomas, Leeza, Bryan, and Kate stepped out.

"There you are," called Kate. She ran over to Lindie Lou, scooped her up, and held her in her arms. "It's time for us to go."

Bryan and Kate said goodbye to Gundula. They followed Leeza, Tomas, and Bella down the hallway toward the exit.

The doorman was waiting. He opened the back of the car pod, lifted their luggage inside, and closed the hatch.

Leeza **hugged** Kate and Lindie Lou. She thanked Kate for the drawings for her new book.

Tomas reached out and shook Bryan's hand. Then they patted each other on the back.

"Where will you go next?" asked Leeza.

"Let me give you a hint. . .," said Bryan.

"In December, we'll be going to a place in Canada to see polar bears. Then we plan to sail across the Hudson Strait to a city called Nuuk. While we're there, we hope to see

glaciers

and the

Northern Lights.

"Wow, it sounds like another amazing adventure," said Leeza.

"I'm sure it will be," replied Bryan.

When the car pod drove away from the Gray Stone Manor, Bryan and Kate waved goodbye. Tomas, Leeza, and the doorman waved, too. Lindie Lou was on Kate's lap. She looked out of the window at Bella and winked.

Bella smiled and winked back.

Kate was singing the Lindie Lou Song.

Lin-die Lou you are cool and your friends think you're a jewel.

La la la La la la la la La la la la la

Lindie Lou Song

Chorus 1
La-la-la,
La-la-la-la-la,
La-la-la-la,
La-la-la.

Verse 1
L-I-N-D-I-E
L-O-U spells
Lindie Lou.

Chorus 2
La-la-la,
La-la-la-la-la,
La-la-la,
La-la.

Verse 2
Lindie Lou,
you are cool,
and your friends
think you're a jewel.

Chorus 2
La-la-la,
La-la-la-la-la,
La-la-la,
La-la.

Verse 3
You are a
very lucky girl,
'cuz you've been
all over the world.

Chorus 2
La-la-la,
La-la-la-la-la,
La-la-la,
La-la.

Verse 4
I can't wait
to see,
where you
take me.

Chorus 2
La-la-la,
La-la-la-la-la,
La-la-la,
La-la.

(Pause)

Chorus 1
La-la-la,
La-la-la-la-la,
La-la-la-la,
La-la-la.

Verse 5
You are my
little Lindie Lou,
and I love you.

Chorus 2
La-la-la,
La-la-la-la-la,
La-la-la,
La-la.

Go to lindielou.com to listen to the "Lindie Lou Song."

Fun Facts

- The first capital of the United States was New York City.

- Central Park was the first public landscaped park in all of the United States.

- The first pizzeria in the United States opened in NYC in 1905.

- There are over 80 museums in NYC. Some of the favorites are:
  1. The Metropolitan Museum of Art;
  2. The American Museum of Natural History;
  3. The 9/11 Memorial Museum;
  4. TheMoMA; Museum of Modern Art.

- There are more than 23,000 restaurants in NYC. You can eat at a different one every day for over 63 years.

- The Brooklyn Bridge is one of the oldest suspension bridges in the United States. It opened in 1883.

- The Statue of Liberty on Liberty Island holds a tablet inscribed with the date of the American Declaration of Independence, July 4th, 1776.

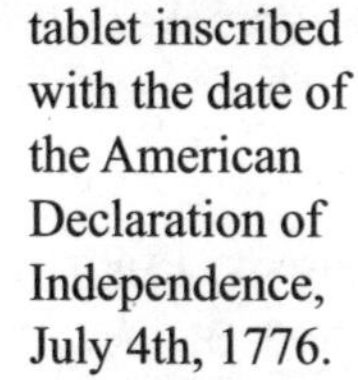

- The Genesee River in the State of New York flows through Rochester and is one of the few rivers in the world that flows south to north.

- Central Park is the most filmed public park in the world. It appears in over 240 feature films.

- The apple is the official state fruit of New York.

New York City, New York • Calendar

January
CHINESE NEW YEAR. This celebration offers several days of free events including the Lunar New Year Flower Market, the Lunar New Year Parade & Festival, and the Firecracker Ceremony and Cultural Festival.

February
WESTMINSTER DOG SHOW. Dog fans come to Madison Square Garden to watch regal canines compete for best in show.

March
NEW YORK INTERNATIONAL CHILDREN'S FILM FESTIVAL. This is an ideal event for the whole family. Come watch animated shorts to full-length films, live-action dramas and engage in youth-oriented films.

April
EARTH DAY. Celebrate the greenest day of the year. Attend one of the many events encouraging locals and visitors to be earth-friendly throughout the year.

May
NINTH AVENUE INTERNATIONAL FOOD FESTIVAL. Taste what current chefs are cooking. Enjoy the 15-blocks featuring various foods from all over the world.

June
MUSEUM MILE FESTIVAL. Nine of the country's finest museums offer free admission into a block party with street performers, activities for kids, and live music.

July

MACY'S FOURTH OF JULY FIREWORKS. Celebrate America's independence from a waterfront view in the city and watch as fireworks light up the skyline.

August

RICHMOND COUNTY FAIR. A Staten Island tradition since 1979. Enjoy circus performers, a petting zoo, visit cartoon characters, and compete in a pie-eating contest.

September

NEW YORK FILM FESTIVAL. This festival brings some of the world's most creative movies to New York City each year. This is the place to see cutting-edge films before they make it big.

October

VILLAGE HALLOWEEN PARADE. This is a lively NYC tradition you don't want to miss. It includes crazy costumed characters, puppets, bands, dancers, and about 2 million attendees. Wear your costume and enjoy!

November

MACY'S THANKSGIVING DAY PARADE. Giant helium-filled character balloons float along a 2.5 mile route and are the focus of this festive parade. Join the 2.5 million fans and help celebrate the day.

December

TIME SQUARE, NEW YEAR'S EVE PARTY. Watch the crystal ball drop in Times Square. Join a million others who have come from all over the world to help celebrate the New Year.

QUICK QUIZ

1. What city does Lindie Lou travel to?

2. Lindie Lou learns about the Legend of the Big Apple. What is she looking for?

3. Tomas and Leeza's dog Bella is a rescue dog. What does this mean?

4. What do Lindie Lou and Bella ride on underneath the city?

5. Who has a message for Lindie Lou? What is the message?

6. Name four places Lindie Lou visits in New York City?

7. How does Lindie Lou find out which direction to go in Central Park?

8. What is the secret of the big apple?

9. Name three of the lessons Lindie Lou learns in this book.

10. What does Gundula write on a piece of paper at the end of the story?

Answers:

(1) New York City (2) Big Apple Tree (3) A dog placed in a home after it has been treated unfairly. (4) subway (5) Gundula; Clues which lead Lindie Lou closer to finding the Big Apple Tree. (6) Gray Stone Manor, Central Park, Times Square, One World Trade Center, Oculus, Pette's Pie Company, Union Square Green Market, Blockhouse, Macy's Parade (7) Saul teaches her how to find north, south, east, and west. (8) friendship (9) You can't tell a secret but you can tell what it is about; apples are good for you; if your right hand faces east...; ask for proof before you trust a stranger; things that are invisible to many, may be visible to some; if you act without thinking you may get into trouble. (10) Believe

Lindie Lou with her Brothers and Sisters

This poster is for sale at
https://lindielou.com/shop.html

Places to go with

New York City, New York

Find links to dog parks, pet-friendly hotels,
restaurants, and dog sitters
on the KIDS tab on our website

https://lindielou.com/places-to-go.html

TEACHERS, LIBRARIANS, AND PARENTS

Enjoy the Lindie Lou Adventure Series

Lindie Lou Adventure Series books are written for kindergarten through third-grade readers. Lindie Lou is a charming puppy who is born in Saint Louis in the first book, adopted by a family in Seattle in the second book, and travels with her family all over the world in the third through twelvth books. The series is often used as a bridge between early chapter books and novels.

Parents and Teachers: The first book was piloted with dozens of educators and hundreds of students before it was published. Pre-K-Grade 3 educators overwhelmingly asked for a series they could use as a read aloud with their primary age students. The series is also being used by teachers with Young Gifted, ELL, High-Low Readers, Emergent Readers and Special Education students through Middle School. **The series supports Reading, Language Arts, Social Studies, Science, Music and Technology Learning Standards.** The books are available in paperback, hardcover, and ebook.

School and Public Librarians have had success using the Lindie Lou Adventure Series and lindielou.com with their classes who are studying series books or doing author studies. Afterschool groups, families who homeschool their children, and Summer Reading Programs have included the series on their "must read" lists. Due to librarian's requests, the books are available in hardcover, paperback, and ebook.

Readers and listeners enjoy the books' large text, colorful illustrations, and creative graphics. As young readers improve their reading skills, the books in the Lindie Lou Adventure Series transform from a colorful read-aloud to an independent read. Readers who excel at a young age will enjoy the age-appropriate storyline. The Lindie Lou Adventure Series is considered a "safe" choice by our distributors. There isn't anything in our books that is threatening, scary, or inappropriate.

Each book includes hints about where Lindie Lou is going, a calendar of events, links for places to go, and a quick quiz. The extra content encourages children to continue learning even when the book is finished. After reading Book 1, *Flying High*, the other books in the series can be read in any order. They are not dependent on one other.

The Lindie Lou website: lindielou.com
The website includes videos of the author reading the first chapter of each book, detailed author information for author studies, the opportunity to video chat or blog with the author for free, downloadable,

projectable, and printable lessons for each book, and the Lindie Lou Song!

Videos found on the Kids page of lindielou.com allow readers to connect with Jeanne Bender personally. She describes meeting the real Lindie Lou for the first time. She talks about how many books will be in the series and where Lindie Lou will be going. Viewers see Lindie Lou traveling with Jeanne, just like Lindie Lou traveled in a carrier in the first book. Videos not found on the website are also available on youtube.com.

Students contact Jeanne Bender to tell her they want to be a writer, they can't wait for her next book to come out, and that they want her to write a book that takes place in their town. Jeanne is especially pleased when readers tell her they want to visit the places Lindie Lou goes to in her books.

Lindie Lou®
Adventure Series

- Book 1: FLYING HIGH

  Flying on an Airplane for the Very First Time

Lindie Lou is a curious puppy who dreams of seeing the world. She lives in a "Puppy Playground" with her brothers and sisters. One day, Lindie Lou learns she is being adopted by a family who lives far away. Soon she is "Flying High" on an airplane for the very first time!

- Book 2: UP IN SPACE

  An Adventure at the Space Needle

Follow Lindie Lou through the city of Seattle, where she meets up with an old friend, meets new friends and learns life lessons along the way. Join in the fun when Lindie Lou discovers Rachel the Pig, sees flying fish, orca whales, and the gum wall. But her biggest adventure awaits... when she goes UP IN SPACE.

- Book 3: HARVEST TIME

  A Celebration on an Organic Farm

Lindie Lou has no idea what an organic farm is like. While visiting Cousin Ronda, she discovers a whole new way of living. Join in the fun! Lindie Lou enjoys the thrill of a hayloft, the challenge of a corn maze, the celebration of the harvest, and the dangers of a combine. Her family and friends play together, solve problems together, even save each other's lives!

- *Book 4: BIG CITY MAGIC*

  Uncover the Secret of the Big Apple

Lindie Lou can hardly wait to see what adventures New York City has to offer. She hears a legend about a Big Apple Tree located somewhere on Manhattan Island. Motivation and persistence drives Lindie Lou on an incredible journey because legend says the tree holds a secret so amazing, so incredible, and so important, it can change her life!

- *Book 5: ON ICE*

  Exploring the Arctic with a Polar Bear Cub

Can you guess where Lindie Lou is going next? She's heading north, where she hopes to see glaciers and Northern Lights. Send your guesses to www.lindielou.com/blog-comments-here.html

About the Author and Illustrator

JEANNE BENDER

Author

Jeanne Bender's journey with Lindie Lou began in 2004 when she adopted "La Petite Lindie Lou Peekaboo" from Joe and Sherry, who live near St. Louis. Throughout Lindie Lou's life, she traveled with Jeanne all over the world.

Bender wrote the *Lindie Lou Song* and then spent three years writing her first book, *Flying High* which was published in 2016 by Pina Publishing, Seattle. Jeanne's second and third books in the series, *Up in Space* and *Harvest Time* were published in 2016 and 2017. *Flying High* (2nd edition) was published in 2018. *Big City Magic*, published in 2019 is the fourth book in the series.

Jeanne and Lindie Lou have visited and presented her books to schools and libraries across the United States and Mexico.

Jeanne's generous spirit compels her to support literacy efforts including Love on a Leash; Reading is Fundamental-Southern California; Literacy Trust; Mission of Hope Homeless Shelter; Wolfner Braille Library; Words Alive; Kenya Works, Africa; Marsh Children's Home, Acapulco, Mexico; Unprison Project sponsored by the Children's Book Council; and hurricane relief projects in Florida and Texas.

Bender lives in Seattle in the summer and San Diego in the winter but considers the world her home.

KATE WILLOWS

Illustrator

Kate Willows has worked in the gaming industry as a concept artist for many years. She teaches college art classes. She also spends time teaching children art online through streaming and on Twitch. She has amassed a large following online and continues to use her influence to spread a love and appreciation for art.

Kate Willows loves drawing and coloring on her computer. She creates all the illustrations for the Lindie Lou Adventure Series on her computer. In her spare time she enjoys playing video games, hiking and collecting plants. She lives in the Columbus, Ohio area with her three cats Nyx, Nico and Nani; and two hamsters Baku and Kiki.